BANDIT

THE PUPPY PLACE

Don't miss any of these other stories by Ellen Miles!

Bandit

Baxter

Bear

Bella

Buddy

Chewy and Chica

Cody

Flash

Goldie

Honey

Jack

Lucky

Maggie and Max

Moose

Muttley

Noodle

Patches

Princess

Pugsley

Rascal

Scout

Shadow

Snowball

Sweetie

Ziggy

BANDIT

ELLEN MILES

SCHOLASTIC INC.
New York   Toronto   London   Auckland
Sydney   Mexico City   New Delhi   Hong Kong

For Larry and Rick—sorry there's no monkey!

No part of this publication may be reproduced, stored in a retrieval system, or transmitted in any form or by any means, electronic, mechanical, photocopying, recording, or otherwise, without written permission of the publisher. For information regarding permission, write to Scholastic Inc., Attention: Permissions Department, 557 Broadway, New York, NY 10012.

ISBN 978-0-545-34834-8

Cover art by Tim O'Brien
Original cover design by Steve Scott

12 11 10   15 16/0

Printed in the U.S.A.   40

First printing, October 2011

CHAPTER ONE

"Yum!" Lizzie Peterson swished a hunk of banana-walnut pancake through the pool of sweet maple syrup on her plate. "Your uncle was right," she told her best friend, Maria, just before she took another bite. "These are the best pancakes I've ever had."

"We always try to stop at Al's on our way to the cabin," said Maria's mother.

Maria's dad nodded in agreement. "It's a tradition, ever since Teo told us about it."

Al's was a truck stop, a place where hungry men and women stopped to eat as they crisscrossed the country in their big rigs, delivering furniture and bananas, lumber and running shoes, baseball bats and kitchen faucets. Maria's uncle Teo was one of those truckers. Lizzie had never met Uncle Teo, but she had heard a lot about him. He was Maria's favorite uncle, and he stayed with the Santiagos whenever he was in the area. He was funny and handsome and the best hugger ever, and he brought Maria excellent presents from his travels; she had a collection of MARIA mini license plates from almost every state. She was still waiting for Alaska and Hawaii, but Uncle Teo had promised she would get them someday.

Lizzie felt so lucky to be on her way to the Santiagos' cabin, up north. She had been there once before, and she'd loved it. The pine trees, the trails through the woods, the secret lake—it was a special place. This time, she and Maria planned to explore the woods beyond the lake, where Mr.

Santiago had told them there was an old apple orchard. Lizzie could hardly wait to get there.

"How much farther is it to the cabin?" she asked. She drew her fork through the puddle of maple syrup, making swoopy white lines.

"About an hour and a half," said Mr. Santiago. "Need some help with those?" He pointed his fork at the big pile of pancakes still left on Lizzie's plate.

Maria had warned Lizzie to order the short stack. "The regular size is huge," she'd said. "You'll never be able to eat it all."

But Lizzie hadn't listened. "I can eat a million pancakes," she'd said. "I'm the pancake champion of my whole family. Nobody can eat more pancakes than me."

Maria had just shrugged. "You always have to make everything into a contest. Go ahead, then. Order whatever you want."

Now Lizzie sat there, feeling like an overstuffed sofa but still determined to show that she was the pancake champion. "That's okay," she told Mr. Santiago. "I can manage." Slowly, she wiped another bite of pancake through the syrup and put it into her mouth. Too bad Buddy wasn't lying under the table, the way he would be at home. Buddy would be happy to secretly help her out with finishing her food.

Buddy was the Petersons' brown and tan puppy, the cutest, most wonderful puppy ever. Of course, it was against family rules to feed Buddy from the table, but sometimes Lizzie just couldn't resist his sweet, soulful brown eyes. Sometimes she would let a tiny scrap of pork chop or a crumb of corn bread fall to the floor. Buddy would gobble it up happily while Mom frowned and shook her head at Lizzie. "It was an accident," Lizzie always claimed. Her younger brother Charles

and her toddler brother the Bean (his real n
was Adam) also sometimes had "accidents."
Lizzie suspected that even her dad slipped the
puppy a bite or two once in a while. Buddy was a
lucky dog.

And Lizzie knew she was lucky, too. Lucky to
have a dog of her own, and lucky to be part of a
family that fostered all kinds of puppies. The
Petersons helped puppies who needed homes, taking care of them until they could find the perfect
forever family for each one. The puppies could be
a lot of work, and it was always hard to give each
one up when the time came, but Lizzie loved
fostering.

Now Lizzie looked down at her plate. Was she
lucky to still have so many pancakes left, even
after she had eaten more than her stomach could
really hold? She burped. "Oops." She covered her
mouth, and she and Maria giggled.

"You really don't have to finish it all if you're full," said Mrs. Santiago. "Maybe we could have the last few bites wrapped up as a special treat for Simba."

Simba was a big, beautiful yellow Lab. He was actually right there with them in the restaurant, under the table at Mrs. Santiago's feet. Maria's mom was blind, and Simba was her guide dog, which meant he was allowed to go everywhere she went. Simba had the best manners of any dog Lizzie had ever known. He never begged, or barked, or jumped up, or ran off with something that didn't belong to him. He just waited, quietly and patiently, always ready to help.

"Well . . . okay," said Lizzie. "I'm sure I could finish, but Simba definitely deserves a treat."

Mr. Santiago called the waitress over and asked for a doggy bag. "It's for a real doggy," he said, pointing to Simba, and the waitress smiled.

She went away, and when she came back she

gave Lizzie a container to put her leftovers in. She also put the check down in front of Mr. Santiago.

"Mom gave me money to pay for all our breakfasts," Lizzie said quickly, pulling some bills out of her pocket. "She said it was so nice of you to take me with you to the cabin, and that I was supposed to insist on paying."

Mr. Santiago smiled. "Well, then. I guess we'll accept, with a big thank-you to your folks. That's very nice."

"Can we go pay?" Maria asked. She leaned over and whispered to Lizzie. "They have free mints up at the cash register."

"Sure," said her mom, and Lizzie and Maria scooted out of their booth.

Lizzie followed Maria, noticing that none of the people they passed looked the way she'd always thought a trucker would look. She'd imagined that Maria's uncle Teo, for example, would be a big guy with lots of tattoos and maybe a shaved head. A tough-looking guy. But all the men and women she saw, leaning into cups of coffee at the counter or squirting ketchup on a cheeseburger and fries, just looked like people you'd run into anywhere.

"See?" Maria said when they got to the cash register, where a gray-haired lady sat on a stool. She pointed at a bowl of red and white striped peppermints.

But Lizzie barely heard her. She was too busy looking at the gray-haired lady. Or, rather, she was looking at the puppy in the lady's arms.

CHAPTER TWO

Lizzie had seen lots and lots of puppies, and every single one of them had been cute. But this puppy? This puppy was *beyond* cute. This puppy was so cute she could hardly stand it. He had a long, silky-looking coat—mostly white with some black patches—and long, floppy ears and a black button nose. His sparkly black eyes peeked back at her, framed by a mask of black fur. "Oh!" Lizzie tugged on Maria's arm. "Look!"

Maria turned and gasped. "What an adorable puppy," she said. "What kind is it?"

Lizzie answered before the lady could say

anything. "It's a Shih Tzu, isn't it?" she asked. Slowly, so she wouldn't scare the puppy, she reached out a hand for it to sniff. Lizzie had seen pictures of Shih Tzus before, but she hadn't paid that much attention. She loved all dogs, she really did. But small dogs? Maybe she loved them just a teensy bit less than she loved big dogs. And Shih Tzus were very, very small. On her "Dog Breeds of the World" poster, she remembered now, it said that the little fur-balls never grew more than a foot tall.

"Shidzoo?" the lady asked, pronouncing it the way Lizzie had. "I guess that's what he is." She looked down at the puppy and shrugged. "That's what the note said, anyway."

"Note?" Lizzie asked. By now she was stroking the puppy's soft, soft fur. The puppy stuck out a tiny pink tongue and licked Lizzie's hand.

The lady sighed. "Somebody left this puppy at the kitchen door this morning. Must have been before four A.M. since Pinky—that's the cook—always gets here at four sharp to open up." She shifted the puppy in her arms.

"Left him?" Lizzie stared at her. "What do you mean?"

"I mean left him," the lady said. "In a lettuce box that they must have found in the Dumpster out back. He was all wrapped up in a red towel, to keep him warm."

Maria's mouth was hanging open. "Why would anybody leave such a cute puppy here?" she asked. "If I had a puppy like that, I would never, never leave him anywhere."

The puppy whimpered, and the lady held him closer. She shook her head. "Some folks have it hard these days," she said. "I think they would have liked to keep him, but—" She reached into the pocket of her green "Eat At Al's" apron and pulled out a piece of paper. She handed it to Lizzie. "Here, read it yourself."

Lizzie unfolded the paper. "'This is Bandit,'" she read out loud. Bandit. What a perfect name, because of the black mask around his eyes. She smiled at the puppy. "Hi, Bandit," she said softly. She still could not get over how cute this puppy was. He looked like a stuffed toy. She wanted to gather him up and hug him and—

"Lizzie, the note!" Maria said. "What does it say?" She craned her neck, trying to read over Lizzie's shoulder.

Lizzie looked back at the note. "'Bandit is a Shih Tzu. He is six months old, and we love our little boy very, very much,'" she read. "'But the vet says he needs a special operation for his heart, and we just can't afford that, not if we also want to feed our kids. So we hope you can find someone who can help, before he gets any sicker.'"

"Why would somebody *do* that?" Maria burst out. "They should have left him at their vet's, or at least at an animal shelter, like Caring Paws. Not at a truck stop."

Lizzie felt the pancakes in her stomach turn to lead. Maria was angry, but Lizzie just felt a wave of sadness washing over her. What if Mom and Dad told her they had to give up Buddy because they couldn't afford his care? "Oh." She closed her eyes for a second. "The poor little guy." When she opened her eyes, Bandit was peering back at her, his shiny black eyes alert and happy.

Hi, there! I bet you want to be my friend. Everybody wants to be my friend.

Lizzie couldn't help smiling at the puppy. He didn't *look* sick. Not at all.

The lady nodded. "It's a shame, all right. I'm not sure how they thought *we* could help, except that we get lots and lots of folks through here every day." She looked down at the puppy in her arms. "I swear, every single person who's seen this peanut this morning has fallen in love with him. I never saw a dog who made friends faster than this one does. I'm sure someone will come along who wants to take this sweetheart home. I sure wish I could, but I don't think my cats would appreciate that."

"I'll take him," Lizzie announced.

"What?" Maria stared at her. "Are you crazy?"

Lizzie shrugged. "He needs help."

"But—but," Maria spluttered. "We're on our way to the cabin, for one thing. He needs a big operation, for another. And your parents—"

Lizzie just nodded. "I'll have to call them." She felt very calm, and very sure that she was the right person to help Bandit. She and her family had helped so many puppies, and this one needed their help most of all. "I'm sure they'll come get me. We're only a half hour or so from home."

"What's going on here?" Maria's father joined them at the cash register. "We should get back on the road." Then he caught sight of the puppy. "Oh, my," he said. "Who's this?"

"That's Bandit," said Lizzie. "My family is going to foster him."

Mr. Santiago raised an eyebrow. "You mean you want to bring him to the cabin with us?"

Lizzie shook her head. "I think it would be better to take him home, if you don't mind waiting for my mom or dad to come pick me up. I hate to miss out on going to the cabin, but this is important. Bandit needs our help."

A few moments later, Lizzie was standing on the restaurant's front steps. "Right," she said into the phone she'd borrowed from Maria's dad. "A puppy. A puppy in trouble. We're at Al's. How soon can you be here?"

CHAPTER THREE

When Lizzie went back inside Al's, she saw Maria and her father still talking to the lady holding Bandit. "Dad's coming to get me," Lizzie told them. "Luckily, he isn't on duty today." Lizzie's dad was a firefighter. "He feels kind of bad about making you wait with me until he gets here."

Mr. Santiago nodded. "That's okay. We're not really on any schedule. I have lots to do up at the cabin, fixing the roof and getting things set for the winter, but we'll manage." He looked over at Bandit and smiled. "Maria and Mrs. Kenyon here have explained everything. This little guy needs help. I'm sure Maria's mom won't mind waiting, either."

17

Lizzie could tell that Mr. Santiago had fallen under Bandit's spell, just like everyone else. She followed Mr. Santiago's gaze. Bandit's eyes sparkled back at her and he gave his head a quick shake.

Hi, there! I knew you couldn't stay away from me for long.

Lizzie felt her heart swell. What was it about this tiny pup? He really was irresistible. Now she noticed the name tag on the lady's apron: VELMA KENYON. "Can I hold him, Mrs. Kenyon?" she asked, reaching out for the pup. She was dying to hug him.

Mrs. Kenyon hesitated. "Ooh, I just hate to let him go," she admitted. "But I guess I'm going to have to hand him over sometime, so it might as well be now." She kissed the top of Bandit's head.

"You sure are a charmer," she told the puppy. "I won't forget you."

Lizzie stepped forward and took Bandit into her arms. He was light as a feather, and so, so soft. He squirmed around just for a moment, nuzzling Lizzie's cheek and breathing his sweet warm puppy breath on her, then settled in comfortably.

Okay. Now what are we doing?

Maria giggled. "It's like he's saying, 'So, what's next?'" she said.

"Maybe what's next is that he should go out for a walk," Lizzie said. Bandit had on a little baby-blue collar with a matching leash attached.

"Good idea. I bet Simba could use a walk, too," Maria's dad said.

Lizzie felt something in her hand. The check from their breakfast. In all the excitement, she'd never paid it. Juggling Bandit carefully, she handed it to Mrs. Kenyon, along with the bills from her pocket. "I got pancakes *and* a puppy," she said. "That's a breakfast to remember."

It seemed like no time at all before Lizzie's dad arrived, pulling into the parking lot in his red pickup. "Well, well, well," he said, as he strode over to the grassy area where Lizzie and Maria were walking Bandit. "What have we here?" He knelt down and let Bandit come over to sniff him.

Lizzie laughed as the tiny pup pulled her along, bounding like a bunny over to Dad.

"What a cutie," Dad said, scooping him up and giving him a kiss on the head. He smiled down at Bandit. Then he looked up at Lizzie, and his expression grew serious. "If this pup really does need a heart operation, we're taking on an awfully big responsibility," he said. "Mom and I agreed to take him, since you seem to feel so strongly about helping him. But it may not be easy."

"I know," said Lizzie. "And thanks, Dad. Thanks for coming to get us."

Mr. Santiago put a hand on Dad's shoulder. "I appreciate it, too. We'd better be shoving off," he said.

"So should we," Dad told Lizzie. "I already called Dr. Gibson, and she said we should bring him straight to her office so she can try to figure out what's wrong with him."

Lizzie still had a hard time believing that there was *anything* wrong with Bandit. He looked and acted perfectly normal. But Dad was right. They had to get him checked out.

Bandit hopped into Dad's pickup as if he'd been riding in it all his life. Lizzie held the puppy snug in her arms as Dad drove to Dr. Gibson's office. Bandit didn't whimper or squirm around at all; he just watched out the window, enjoying the scenery. Every so often Lizzie kissed the top of his head. She had never thought she could fall in love so fast—especially with a little dog.

Dr. Gibson was waiting when they arrived. "Aha," she said, when she saw Bandit. "Here's our little patient." Smiling, she lifted him from Lizzie's arms. "Oh, aren't you the cutest?" she said, rubbing noses with him.

The vet tech at the front desk giggled.

"What?" Dr. Gibson asked.

"I've just never seen you act quite like that around a dog," she said. "All kissy-poo, I mean."

Dr. Gibson shrugged. "It only takes a second to see that this guy is something special," she said. She turned to Lizzie and her dad. "I've asked Carolyn here to make some calls to all the vets in the area, in case someone knows this pup and has treated him. I sure would like to see his file. But meanwhile, I'll give him a good checkup and get back to you as soon as I can." She started to walk back toward her examining rooms.

"Wait," said Lizzie. "You mean we have to leave him here?"

Dr. Gibson turned. "I think that's best. It may take me some time to figure out what's going on with him. And I need to make a call to an old friend of mine from veterinary school. He's a surgeon who works in a fancy animal hospital in Boston, and he may be able to help us if Bandit really does need an operation. Anyway, I promise to call you as soon as I know."

Lizzie ran over to give Bandit one last kiss on the head. She could hardly stand to leave him, but Dr. Gibson was right. The most important thing right now was to find out exactly what was wrong with him.

At home, Lizzie tried to keep busy, playing some of her favorite games with Buddy. She put her hands behind her back and tucked a small treat into her left hand. Then she brought both hands out in front. "Which hand, Buddy?" she asked.

Wagging his tail hard, Buddy sniffed both hands carefully. Then he nudged her left hand with his nose.

"Good boy!" Lizzie cried, opening up her hand.

Later, they were playing tag in the backyard when she heard the phone ring. She dashed inside to grab it before anyone else could. Maybe it was Dr. Gibson.

But it was only Maria. "How's Bandit?" she asked.

"I don't know yet," Lizzie said. "I'm waiting to hear from the vet." She explained that they'd had to leave the puppy at Dr. Gibson's office. "How's the cabin?" she asked, feeling a pang of longing for the tall pines and the cozy fireplace.

"Okay, but kind of boring without you," said Maria.

"I'll come next time. Anyway, I better get off the phone in case Dr. Gibson is trying to reach us.

Call me again tomorrow—I should know more by then."

Finally, an hour later while Lizzy was trying to teach Buddy to bark on command, the phone rang again. This time, it was Dr. Gibson.

"Lizzie?" she asked. Her voice sounded serious. "You can come get Bandit and take him home with you."

Lizzie's heart lifted for a moment. "That's great!" she said. "But—?"

Dr. Gibson paused. "Maybe I should talk to your parents," she said.

"You can tell me!" said Lizzie. She thought she might die right that moment if she didn't know the truth.

"Well," said Dr. Gibson. "What it said in that note was true. Bandit does need heart surgery. And he needs it soon."

CHAPTER FOUR

It didn't take long for the rest of Petersons to fall in love with Bandit, just like Dad and Lizzie had. For the rest of that weekend, Mom whispered baby talk to the puppy as she fed him his meals. Dad lay down on the rug and let Bandit climb all over him. Charles made a special place mat for Bandit, colored with pictures and sayings like WELCOME, BANDIT! And the Bean followed Bandit everywhere, laughing his googly laugh every time the puppy licked his hands or face.

Lizzie wondered if Buddy would get jealous, but he didn't. He obviously loved Bandit as much as everyone else did, and the two puppies spent hours playing. Buddy seemed to understand that he had to be careful with his new friend.

Lizzie laughed as she and the rest of her family watched them wrestle gently on the living-room floor on Sunday afternoon.

"Look, Buddy's pretending to let Bandit win," she said, as the tiny black-and-white puppy stood over the sturdy brown one. Buddy grinned a doggy grin up at Bandit, whose eyes were bright with excitement. Bandit wagged his tail victoriously.

I may be small, but I'm mighty!

"Aww," said Dad. "Good boy, Buddy."

"Are you sure it's okay to let them play like that?" Mom asked. "What about Bandit's heart?"

Lizzie and Dad both nodded. "Dr. Gibson said it was fine," Lizzie told her mom. "He isn't supposed to tear around outside, but he doesn't seem to want to do that anyway. And she said he might get tired easily and need lots of naps." The vet had explained to Lizzie and her dad that Bandit was born with a problem in his heart—something Lizzie didn't quite understand that had to do with valves. It wasn't uncommon, according to Dr. Gibson, and it wasn't usually too hard to fix, at least not for a surgeon with experience. But if it didn't get fixed, or if the operation did not go well, Bandit could die.

Lizzie went over to pick Bandit up. Immediately, he forgot all about playing and squirmed comfortably into her lap, gazing up at her with his shiny black eyes. "You're a cuddle-bug, aren't you?" Lizzie asked him.

Sure, whatever you say. Just keep on petting me.

Dad came over to pet Bandit, too. He shook his head. "I tried to resist, but I can't help myself. I just love this dog."

"Why would you try to resist?" Charles asked. He and the Bean were lying on the floor, petting Buddy.

"Well." Dad cleared his throat. "I mean, maybe it's not a good idea to get too attached to a dog who could—who might not—" He looked helplessly at Mom.

"Who might not stay with us for too long," Mom said quickly, and Charles and the Bean both nodded. They knew what it meant to be a foster family; you had to give up puppies even if you came to care for them very much.

But Lizzie knew that was not what Dad had meant. She knew that he was worried that Bandit might not make it. If he didn't get that operation soon . . . She closed her eyes. She didn't even want to think about that.

The operation was going to be very, very expensive. The night before, when they had gone to pick up Bandit, Dr. Gibson told Lizzie and Dad how much it would cost. When Dad's eyes bugged out, Dr. Gibson added, "And that's half-price. My vet-school buddy down in Boston said he would give us a break because of Bandit's circumstances."

Lizzie was trying hard to think of ways to raise money, for the operation and for Bandit's trip to Boston. She'd written a few things down on a piece of paper in her dog scrapbook, a three-ring binder she had begun to keep with photos and descriptions of all the dogs her family had fostered. On the front of the notebook she had made a collage of all the cutest puppy pictures she could find. Buddy's picture was right in the middle, of course.

Bake sale? she had written under the heading *BANDIT FUND-RAISING IDEAS*, even though she knew that her family would end up eating most of the cookies she would make to sell. *Raffle?* came next, even though she couldn't think of anything to sell raffle tickets for. She didn't know how to make a quilt, like the one they raffled off every year at the library, and she couldn't afford to buy a shiny new bike for a prize. *Save allowance?* was the last thing on her pathetic list, and as Lizzie looked at it she sighed. It would take her until she was about fifty-three years old to save up enough money for a heart operation.

Lizzie was just thinking that maybe Maria would have some ideas after she got home from the cabin, when the phone rang. It was Maria. "We got home early," Maria said. "Actually, we came home early on purpose—because we couldn't wait to see Bandit again! How is he? Can we come over? Uncle Teo just showed up for a visit, and he wants to meet the 'truck stop dog.'"

Lizzie put her hand over the phone as she checked with her parents. Then she spoke to Maria again. "Sure," she said. "We'll fill you in on all the news when you get here."

Mom went to put the kettle on for tea while

Lizzie and Charles helped Dad straighten up the living room. Bandit followed Lizzie everywhere, trotting along behind her as she tidied the coffee table and plumped up sofa pillows. Charles tried to put all of Buddy's toys into a basket, but no matter how fast he worked Buddy worked faster, pulling them back out one by one and shaking them in his mouth as he ran around the room.

When the doorbell rang, Lizzie ran to open the door. There on the porch stood Maria, her parents, and Simba, along with a big, burly man with a shaved head and—Lizzie spotted them right away—tattoos on both of his huge, muscular forearms.

"Hi, Lizzie," said Maria. "This is my uncle Teo."

CHAPTER FIVE

"There he is," Maria squealed, pushing past Lizzie to run toward Bandit. She plopped down on the floor with him, scooped him up, and nuzzled her nose into his neck. "Ooh, he's even cuter than I remembered."

Lizzie, still standing at the door, remembered her manners. "Come on in," she said to Maria's parents and her uncle. Mom and Dad came into the living room to say hello, and soon everyone was standing in a circle around Bandit, cooing over him.

"Oh, the poor little thing," said Mrs. Santiago, when she heard that it was true about him needing a heart operation.

Mr. Santiago knelt down to pet Bandit. "You're gonna be just fine, big guy," he said softly.

Now Bandit lay on his back, squirming happily and waving his front paws in the air. Charles, Maria, Lizzie, and the Bean sat on the floor near Bandit, taking turns petting him.

Yes! I'm the center of attention. This is how I like it. This is how it should always be.

Lizzie glanced up at Uncle Teo. He stood with his arms folded and a slight smile on his face as he watched the others hover over Bandit. Lizzie nudged Maria and raised her eyebrows.

"Don't you like Bandit, Uncle Teo?" Maria asked.

Uncle Teo grinned and shrugged. "He's okay, I guess. I've just never been into little dogs. Plus, he's just kind of . . ." He held out his hands. "I don't know. Fluffy."

Lizzie noticed that when Uncle Teo moved his arms, his tattoos moved, too. The one on his left forearm was of a group of palm trees, and they looked as if they were waving in the wind. That was kind of cool.

"How about some coffee or tea?" Mom asked, and the grown-ups all followed her into the kitchen. The Bean toddled after them, calling out "Cookie for the Bean?" in his most pleading voice.

"So," said Maria, when they'd left, "what about his operation?"

Lizzie sighed. "Charles and I made a list of all the things we'll need to do to help Bandit." She grabbed her notebook and read aloud. "'Number One: Take good care of him until he gets his operation.' That's easy. We're used to taking care of puppies. 'Number Two: Figure out how he's going to get down to Boston and back.' That's a lot harder."

"No, it isn't," yelled someone from the

kitchen. "I'll take care of that. Transportation is my job."

Uncle Teo! Lizzie grinned at Maria. Her uncle really was a good guy, even if he hadn't fallen in love with Bandit like everyone else.

"I wonder if he'll take him in his big rig," Charles whispered.

Lizzie shook her head. "No, silly," she said. "I really doubt that truckers are allowed to have dogs with them on the road."

"Actually," said Maria, "lots of them do. Dogs are good company when you're driving for hours a day. Uncle Teo used to have a really sweet pit bull mix named Roscoe, but he had to give him away because Roscoe kept getting carsick."

Charles stuck out his tongue at Lizzie. Then he got up and headed into the kitchen, just in case Mom had decided to hand out cookies, Lizzie guessed. Buddy jumped up and trotted after him, probably for the same reason.

"Oh," said Lizzie. "Well, that's great, then. Now all we have to do is figure out how to do Number Three on the list: 'Raise twenty-five hundred dollars.'"

Maria's mouth fell open. She stared at Lizzie.

"That means two thousand, five hundred dollars," Lizzie explained.

"I know what it means," said Maria. "I just can't believe what I'm hearing. That's a lot of money."

"Dr. Gibson said we don't have to raise it all at once," Lizzie told her friend. "She went ahead and scheduled Bandit's surgery for next week, and we can pay afterward." She reached out to pet Bandit's soft ears. "But we're going to have to figure out how to raise all that money." She opened her notebook again and read the fund-raising ideas she'd written down. They sounded even stupider this time.

"What about some kind of dog business?"

Lizzie looked up to see Uncle Teo leaning in the doorway. He'd been listening. She felt her face flush and knew she was blushing. "What do you mean?" she asked him.

"Well, I know Maria loves dogs, and from what she tells me you're even more dog-crazy than she is. There must be some way to make money around that."

Lizzie thought for a moment. "We did have a dog wash one time, when my family was fostering Chewy and Chica, a pair of Chihuahua puppies. It was fun, but it sure was messy—and it didn't raise that much money."

"Well, how about walking dogs? Aren't there people around here who might need their dogs walked while they're at work?" Uncle Teo gestured when he said "around here," and the palm trees waved in the wind again.

Lizzie and Maria stared at each other. Why hadn't they thought of that?

"Uncle Teo, that's a great idea." Maria jumped up to hug him.

Uncle Teo shrugged modestly. "I'm an idea man," he said. "I have a few other ideas about raising money for that scamp's operation. I'll let you know how those turn out." He winked, then turned to go back into the kitchen.

"A dog-walking business," said Lizzie. "It's so perfect. What should we charge? A dollar a walk? Two dollars?" She started to write things down in her notebook. "How about three dollars for a twenty-minute walk? Does that sound fair? And—hey!—I have the perfect name. We'll call ourselves AAA Plus Dog Walkers. I read somewhere that AAA is a good business name because it'll be the first listing in the phone book. Plus it sounds good, like we're the best. People would want to trust their dogs to the best, right?" She looked up at Maria. Why was her friend so quiet? Oops. Maybe because she had been talking non-stop, so Maria had not had the chance to speak. "Right?" she asked again.

"Sure, I guess so," said Maria. "I like everything you said. Except—maybe the name. I think I'd rather call our business something a little more . . . more interesting. After all, it's not like we're going to be in the phone book, anyway. We're just going to make posters, right? Or go around and knock on doors to introduce ourselves? So we could be called, like, Dynamic Dog Walkers. Or something."

"I still like AAA Plus," Lizzie said, folding her arms.

Maria was quiet for a moment. "How about this?" she finally said. "Since you'll probably be walking dogs in your neighborhood, and I'll be walking them in my neighborhood, we can each have our own business, with its own name."

Lizzie stuck out her hand. "It's a deal," she said, smiling. She was already sure that her dog-walking business would raise way more money than Maria's.

"Just one thing," added Maria. "Can you please, please try not to make this into a contest?"

CHAPTER SIX

When Lizzie got home from school the next day, she flung her backpack onto the bench in the front hall and plopped down on the ground to hug and kiss Buddy and Bandit, who had run to greet her. "Hi, sweeties," she said, as she ruffled Buddy's ears and kissed Bandit's nose. "I can't hang around today; I have a business to start. But Charles is going to take good care of you, and walk you, and play with you." She glanced up at her brother, who had come in just behind her. "Right?" she asked.

Charles nodded. "As long as you don't forget that you owe me."

"I won't forget," said Lizzie. She and Charles usually split the responsibility of taking care of Buddy and any foster puppies staying at the house. But now she had another responsibility: raising money for Bandit's operation. She needed Charles to do more than his share of puppy care for a while. So she had promised him one-fourth of any Halloween candy she got. She might be sorry about that later, but Halloween was still a long way away. Right now she cared more about getting her dog-walking business going.

She had spent the night before making up some flyers. AAA Plus Dog Walkers, the posters said. The porfessional, responsable choice for animal care. You can trust us with your pet. She had colored all the posters with pictures of dogs of every breed, copied from her "Dog Breeds of the World" poster, and decorated them with puppy stickers. Each flyer had her name and phone number on it. Afternoon dog-walking service: Three dollars for twenty-minute walk.

Lizzie was very pleased with her flyers. She especially liked the way she had drawn long leashes around the borders of each piece of paper, as one more eye-grabbing decoration.

Now she kissed both puppies one more time, then picked up the stack of flyers and shoved them into her backpack. She yelled good-bye to Charles and Mom as she followed Dad out to his truck. He had insisted on coming with her this first day, since she would be knocking on strangers' doors. Lizzie didn't mind. Probably people would take her more seriously if they knew she was a firefighter's daughter.

"Let's start over on Sunset," she told her dad as they backed down the driveway.

"I thought you and Maria were each looking for customers in your own neighborhoods," said Dad. "Isn't Sunset Avenue closer to where she lives?"

Lizzie looked out the window. "Not really. Well, it's kind of on the edge of both our neighborhoods," she said. "Anyway, I was thinking I could start knocking on doors over there and work my way back toward home."

Dad shrugged. "You're the boss," he said.

It only took five minutes to drive over to Sunset. When they arrived, Lizzie asked Dad to pull over for a second as she eyed the houses on the block. She noticed a big brick house with white columns and a long walkway leading up to the front door. When Lizzie saw the white picket fence enclosing the whole yard, she guessed there might be a dog in the family. "I'm going to try that one," she said. "Will you wait here?"

When Dad agreed, she got out of the truck, carrying her backpack. She took a deep breath, pushed open the gate, and marched up the walk. For a moment, she wished that Maria were marching next to her. It would have been a lot easier—and probably more fun—to do this together. But there was no time to think about that now: She was at the front door. She rang the doorbell. Instantly, a dog began to bark inside. Deep, loud woofs echoed through the house. Yes. A home with a dog. Just what she'd been hoping for. Then Lizzie heard footsteps. "Hush, Atlas!" someone said.

A woman opened the door, struggling to hold a huge, slobbering golden retriever. "Hello?" she said, giving Lizzie a curious look.

"Hi," said Lizzie, suddenly remembering that she had forgotten to take a flyer out of her back-pack. "I'm Lizzie. Lizzie Peterson. I'm starting a dog-walking business and—"

Just then, Atlas wrenched himself loose and made a dash for the door.

"No! Wait!" yelled the woman.

Lizzie stepped forward and grabbed the dog's collar. "Gotcha," she said. Atlas stopped short. Lizzie smiled. "Where do you think you're going, buddy?" She petted his big head. "Sit," she told him.

Atlas sat. He looked up at Lizzie.

"Wow," said the woman. "You're good. Did you say you're a dog walker? Atlas sure could use more exercise than I can give him, to burn off all that energy. And you look like you could handle him. When can you start?"

Lizzie grinned. "How does tomorrow sound?"

After that, it was easy. Lizzie talked to people who were in their yards with their dogs. Dad helped her put up flyers on telephone poles, and they stuck them in people's mailboxes. They stopped by a small park where people took their dogs to run and play together. It took them all afternoon to work their way back to their own neighborhood, but by the time Lizzie collapsed on the couch at home she had signed up six everyday clients, plus she had the names of three more people who might be interested in a once-in-a-while walk.

Lizzie pulled Bandit onto her lap as she sorted through the notes she had made on the dogs she would be walking. Each dog had his or her own index card, with lots of information. She had interviewed each client carefully to make sure she knew as much as possible about the dogs she would be caring for. Name, breed, age, likes and dislikes — it was all there.

"Tank should be fun," she told Bandit. "He's a young German shepherd with lots of energy. And then there's Scruffy, the Morkie. Isn't that a funny breed name? He's a mix of Maltese and Yorkie.

His owner said he barks a lot. He's only a tiny bit bigger than you are."

The bouncy black-and-white pup on her lap stretched his neck up and licked Lizzie's chin.

Just remember, I'm the most important dog.

"Don't worry, I won't forget about you." Lizzie laughed, stroking his soft fur. She went back to her notes. "Then we have Ginger. She's kind of old. I think she's mostly beagle, with some basset mixed in. And Dottie the Dalmatian, who's a little deaf, so I have to use hand signals with her, and Maxx the miniature Doberman pinscher. He's a handful, for sure. And of course there's Atlas." Lizzie sighed, putting her head back on the couch. How was she going to manage?

She had asked each owner if their dogs got along with other dogs, and all but Ginger's owner had said yes. That meant she could walk the other five all together, which would save lots of time. Still, picking them all up and getting them all back home was going to take some planning. But she could handle it—couldn't she?

CHAPTER SEVEN

Later that night, just before bedtime, Maria called. "Guess what?" she blurted out, as soon as Lizzie picked up the phone. "I have three clients! Three dogs, times five walks a week, times three dollars a walk. That's forty-five dollars a week. We'll raise the money in no time. How about you? Did you get any clients?"

"A few," said Lizzie, grinning to herself as she pumped a fist. Yes! Starting out over on Sunset had really paid off. She had twice as many clients as Maria, so she'd be earning twice as much money. That was—she did the math—ninety dollars a week! Fantastic. But she kept quiet. She didn't want to hear Maria tell her she had made this dog-walking thing into a contest. Even though she possibly, maybe, sort of, kind of . . . had.

Quickly, she changed the subject. "You should see Bandit. He is so cute. He's sleeping on my bed right now, but before dinner he was playing with Buddy's big stuffed teddy bear. The bear was almost bigger than he was, but Bandit carried it all over the house. I guess he finally tired himself out."

"Awww," said Maria. "Little Bandit. Hey, you know what's weird? I think somebody else around here might have started a dog-walking business, too. When I went over to Sunset to try to get more clients, people kept telling me they were all set. I wonder who that could be?"

"Um," said Lizzie. It was time to change the subject again. "I think I hear my dad calling. I better go." She hung up, feeling a wave of queasiness in her stomach. She should have just told

Maria that *she* was the person walking dogs on Sunset. But did it really matter who was walking which dogs? After all, the main thing was to raise money for Bandit's operation. Bandit! She ran upstairs to her room to find the puppy still asleep on her bed. He had found the most comfortable spot, cozied up between her two pillows. "Bandit," she cooed, curling up next to him. He yawned, a sleepy pink yawn, and kissed her on the cheek.

Hi, there. It's about time somebody found me and gave me some attention.

Then he yawned again. His eyelids drooped, and a moment later he was fast asleep.

Sleep did not come so easily to Lizzie that night. She kept going over her client list in her mind, trying to figure out the best route to take as she picked up each dog. And every time she thought about her clients on Sunset, she felt a twinge in her tummy.

The next day, Lizzie set out right after school. She had decided to head over to Sunset first, pick up Atlas, then work her way back toward her own neighborhood, picking up dogs along the way. When she'd picked up Maxx, the dog who lived nearest to her house, she would walk all of them back toward Sunset to return Atlas, then drop off the other dogs as she headed home. That way, each dog would get a nice long walk. Then, when she was done with the group walk, she'd have to walk Ginger on her own. But that would be easy. Ginger lived just down the street and Mrs. Davis, her owner, said she didn't like to go for long walks. Mom and Dad had seemed doubtful when Lizzie explained her plan, but she was sure she could manage.

It took a lot longer to walk over to Atlas's house than Lizzie had imagined. When she arrived, the big golden retriever was raring to go. She could barely get his leash clipped on before he dashed out the door, dragging her down the walk. "Whoa, whoa!" she yelled. "Slow down, Atlas." She reeled him in and told him to heel. He looked up at her with a happy grin and did exactly what she'd asked, sticking to her left side like glue. Atlas really could behave well, as long as you reminded him to.

Before she and Atlas had even walked the three blocks to her next client's house, Lizzie was glad she'd remembered to stick a bunch of plastic bags in her backpack. Picking up poop was not her favorite part of this job, but she knew it had to be done.

The next dog she picked up was Scruffy, the Morkie. He was adorable, but he turned out to be a dawdler. The little dog stopped at every bush to pee and halted in his tracks whenever he saw a squirrel or cat that needed barking at.

Tank's owner had left the back door unlocked, with a note telling Lizzie where to find his leash and halter. Unfortunately, the halter was not where it was supposed to be, so Lizzie just clipped his leather leash onto his collar and hoped for the best. "Whoa!" she yelled as Tank pulled her *and* the other dogs down the street. This young German shepherd was even stronger than Atlas, but unlike the obedient golden retriever, Tank did not pay one bit of attention when she told him to heel.

For the next few blocks Lizzie thought she was going to be pulled in half as Tank and Atlas surged forward and Scruffy hung back. For a tiny dog, Scruffy was surprisingly strong.

By the time Lizzie stopped to pick up Dottie the Dalmatian, she was already beginning to think

Mom and Dad had been right. Maybe she *couldn't* walk five dogs at once. Fortunately, Dottie was good on the leash—but she did not get along with the other dogs as well as her owner had said she would. She seemed to like Scruffy, but she growled every time Tank or Atlas came near her, lifting her lip and baring her teeth. "No, Dottie," Lizzie yelled every time Dottie growled. But since Dottie was deaf, that didn't do much good. Lizzie just had to try to keep her away from the bigger dogs, which was not easy. All four dogs wove back and forth, tangling their leashes and nearly tripping Lizzie with every step.

Lizzie must have looked frazzled by the time she knocked on the door of the house where Maxx the mini–Doberman pinscher lived. "Are you okay?" asked his owner, Ms. Federico. "Maxx can wait until later if you want to drop some of those other dogs off first." Lizzie assured her that she could manage. "Okay, try to keep him from barking and jumping up," Ms. Federico said as she handed Maxx's leash to Lizzie. "Those are two habits of his we are trying to change."

"Sure," said Lizzie. But Maxx was like a jumping bean. A noisy jumping bean. His feet barely touched the ground as he boing-boinged all over the sidewalk, barking nonstop and jumping up on Lizzie and the other dogs.

Lizzie walked back toward Sunset as quickly as she could, stopping every few feet to untangle leashes, clean up poop, wipe drool off her pants, or let a dog sniff or pee. It was a relief to drop off Atlas, then Scruffy. Tank and Maxx barked at each other for three straight blocks after that, but Dottie, being deaf, didn't seem bothered. By the time Lizzie made it back to Maxx's house, she was exhausted. As she walked up the steps to her own house after dropping him off, she shook her head. Tomorrow, she would have to do things differently.

Walking five dogs at once was much harder than she had expected.

Lizzie stopped on the top step. Five dogs? She had six clients. She smacked her forehead. Ginger! She still had one more dog to walk.

CHAPTER EIGHT

The owner, founder, and only employee of AAA Plus Dog Walkers had a long, hard week of work. But by the end of the week, Lizzie had to admit that she was learning a lot.

On Wednesday, the second day of her dog-walking business, she had tried giving each dog a separate twenty-minute walk. That made things a lot easier—no more tangled leashes—but it took a lot longer, too. Six dogs times twenty minutes, plus pickups and dropoffs and walking between clients' homes: that added up to well over two hours of dog walking, not exactly what she had bargained for. It didn't leave much time for homework, let alone playing with Bandit.

On Thursday, Lizzie had tried different combinations of dogs. She discovered that she could walk Atlas and Maxx at the same time, and Dottie and Scruffy were a good pair, too. And once she found Tank's halter, she could walk him with either of the other two pairs of dogs.

Ginger was a different story. Ginger had to be walked all by herself—not because she didn't get along with other dogs, or pulled too hard, or barked too loudly. No, Ginger was just plain slow. It took the whole twenty minutes just to get her around the block. She ambled along, stopping every few steps to sniff. When Lizzie tried to hurry her, Ginger stood her ground, planting her feet and stiffening her short, stocky legs. Sometimes, no matter how hard Lizzie tugged, she could not get Ginger moving.

"Did I tell you what Ginger did on Friday?" Lizzie asked Maria. It was Sunday now, and she was at her friend's house. She had brought Bandit over, and the two girls had been playing with the puppy all day, giving him lots of love every minute since they knew he would soon be gone. Lizzie could hardly stand to think about it, but any minute now Uncle Teo would stop by to pick up the puppy. He and Bandit would leave for Boston before dawn the next morning, and Bandit would have his operation first thing Monday.

Neither of the girls wanted to talk about that. It was easier to talk about silly Ginger. "She sat down in the middle of the block and refused to go one step farther," Lizzie told her friend.

"What did you do?" Maria asked.

"Finally, I gave up and let her turn around. She headed straight for home, dragging me along." Lizzie shook her head. Ginger was frustrating, but she was a sweet old girl and Lizzie never yelled at her. Lizzie never yelled at any of the dogs. How could you be mad at a dog because she was acting like a dog?

Lizzie reached over to pet Bandit. "He's so sweet," she said. "Mrs. Kenyon was right. Everybody who meets this dog falls in love with him."

"Except for Uncle Teo." Maria laughed. "He's the only one who can resist." She held Bandit up and rubbed noses with him, making kissy noises. "What a good little boy. What a sweetie." She turned to Lizzie. "I can't believe we haven't found Bandit a home yet. Somebody must want to adopt this smoochie-pie."

Bandit licked her cheek and wagged his fluffy tail.

That's right. Who wouldn't love me? I'm a sweetheart.

"I know," said Lizzie. She picked up one of the flyers she'd made about Bandit. *Adorable Shih Tzu seeks Loving Family,* it said. Under the headline was an incredibly cute picture of Bandit, staring back at the camera with his shiny black button eyes. And underneath that, there was some more information about Bandit, including the fact that he would soon be having major surgery.

"What's that?" Lizzie asked now, jumping up to run to the window. She could have sworn she heard the rumble of a truck, but when she looked outside, the street was empty. When would Uncle Teo get there?

Lizzie sat back down and looked at the flyer again. She could guess why none of her dog-walking clients, or any of the other people who had seen the flyer, wanted to adopt Bandit. "It's probably the surgery thing," she said. "Everybody's afraid to get too attached to a dog who might not make it."

"Don't say that." Maria put her hands over

Bandit's ears, as if he could understand what Lizzie was saying.

Lizzie shook her head. "But Dr. Gibson told us—"

"I don't care what she told you," said Maria, hugging the black-and-white puppy to her chest. "Bandit is going to make it. Not only that, he'll be better than ever. The operation is going to work perfectly." Lizzie saw tears in Maria's eyes. She knew that Maria would have loved to adopt Bandit, but Simba was the only pet in the Santiago family and always would be.

"Okay, okay," Lizzie said, holding up her hands. "You're right. He's going to be just fine." She felt tears prickling at the back of her own eyes. Bandit just *had* to pull through. She didn't know what she would do if she never got to hug him again, or watch him trot through a room with his sweet little head held high. She was just as attached as

Maria was, and it wasn't going to be easy to say good-bye to Bandit when Uncle Teo arrived.

Maria sighed and lay back on her bed. "I'm tired," she said. "It's hard work, walking dogs every day."

"I know," Lizzie said. "You wouldn't believe what happened at Caring Paws yesterday." That was the animal shelter where Lizzie volunteered every Saturday afternoon. "I was hoping to work at the front desk, or even clean out litter boxes in the cat room. Anything but walk dogs. But guess what? The person who usually exercises the dogs didn't show up, and I had to walk twelve of them."

Maria laughed, but Lizzie groaned, remembering. Yes, she thought, she had learned a lot that week. The only thing she hadn't learned was how to tell Maria the truth about how many dogs she was walking. She had only told her about Ginger,

Scruffy, and Maxx, not about the three other dogs over in the Sunset neighborhood.

Maria had begged her not to make this dog-walking thing into a contest. But Lizzie hadn't listened. Lizzie *had* made it into a contest—and she had won, too. Now there was no way to tell Maria without sounding as if she were gloating about it—and without confessing that she had been the one who signed up all the clients over on Sunset.

The funny thing was, winning the contest had not made Lizzie happy. Six dogs was too many for her to handle by herself. She was in over her head, and she knew it was her own fault. Next time she started a business, maybe she wouldn't insist on doing it her way. Next time, maybe she and Maria could work together.

She reached over to pet Bandit, who was still cuddled in Maria's arms. She was stroking his

silky ears when she heard a rumbling noise outside. This time, she was sure of it. She ran to the
window and pulled aside the curtain to peep out.
There, pulled right up in front of the house, was
the biggest, shiniest truck she had ever seen. "I
think Uncle Teo's here," she said.

CHAPTER NINE

"Wow!" said Lizzie a few minutes later. She could hardly believe her eyes. "This is awesome." She and Maria and Maria's dad had gone outside to greet Uncle Teo and help get Bandit settled in the truck. Climbing up into the high cab had been tricky, but Lizzie had watched the way Maria swung up the metal stairs and copied her. It was cool to be way up high in the cab of a big rig. Lizzie had been fascinated by the big front seats, the giant steering wheel, and the windshield as big as a picture window. Then Maria had pulled aside a curtain behind the front seats, revealing a tiny room complete with a bed, bookshelves, cabinets, and a mini-fridge.

"A person could practically live in here," said Lizzie.

"A person practically does," said Uncle Teo with a grin, after he'd swept Maria into a bear hug. "When a person is on a long cross-country trip, that is. I've slept back here many a night. It's just as comfortable as my bed at home."

Mr. Santiago stuck his head into the secret room. "Is this where Bandit will be riding?" He held the black-and-white pup in his arms.

Uncle Teo nodded. "I'm all set for Mr. Fluffy. See?" he asked, waving a hand toward the back. Lizzie spotted a small dog crate tucked next to the bed, complete with toys, food and water dishes, and a comfy-looking red plaid cushion. "I found all of Roscoe's old things and set him up. He can snooze back here while we're driving down to Boston."

Lizzie took Bandit from Mr. Santiago and knelt

down by the crate. "Here you go, sweetie," she said, settling him inside it on the red cushion.

Bandit went into the crate but did not lie down. He sat looking up at Lizzie with his bright button eyes.

Now what? Can we go back out now?

"Ohh," Lizzie sighed. She could hardly stand to say good-bye to Bandit. He didn't even know that he was going to the hospital, to have a big operation. The poor guy, all alone in the big city.

She felt a hand on her shoulder. "Don't worry, Lizzie," said Uncle Teo, as if he'd read her mind. "I promise to take good care of him. I have the day off tomorrow, and I won't leave the animal hospital until I know the fluffball is okay."

Lizzie nodded. "Thanks," she whispered. She reached in to pet Bandit. "Lie down, now. Be a good boy," she told him. She petted his silky ears one more time, and Bandit licked her hand.

Maria knelt down beside her and petted Bandit, too.

"Okay, girls," said Mr. Santiago. "Uncle Teo has to get going."

Lizzie and Maria each kissed Bandit one more time. Then they went back out into the cab of the truck, opened the door, and climbed down onto the sidewalk. Lizzie looked up at the truck, which was shiny green with a yellow lightning bolt painted across the door. T. SANTIAGO said the sign in white lettering under the door handle, LONG-HAUL TRUCKING.

"Look, Lizzie!" said Maria, tugging on her sleeve. She pointed to the window. "Bandit looks like he's going to drive *himself* to Boston." There was the black-and-white pup, sitting on Uncle Teo's lap. He must have popped right out of his crate and jumped into the driver's seat.

Uncle Teo opened the window. "I had a feeling this might happen," he said. "Just like my dog Roscoe. He always wanted to ride up front so he could keep an eye on where we were going." He held up a tangle of red nylon webbing. "I've got this harness, so I can strap him safely into the passenger seat. He'll be fine."

Lizzie and Maria watched and waited as Uncle Teo buckled the harness around Bandit, settling him into the front seat on top of a pillow so he could watch out the window. They waved at him. "Bye, Bandit!" they called as Uncle Teo started up the truck. "Bye-bye!"

At school the next day, Lizzie yawned over her vocabulary worksheet. She had not gotten much sleep the night before. She was too worried about Bandit. He might be having his operation right now, this very moment, as she was drawing a line between the word "affectionate" and the definition "having or showing fond feelings." She couldn't stop thinking about Bandit. Would he make it through the operation? How long would it take him to recover from it? How soon would she be able to see him again? And how would she ever find a forever home good enough for this special puppy?

She gazed at another vocabulary word without really seeing it. Instead of connecting words to definitions, she began to draw pictures of Bandit's face all around the margins of her paper.

At the desk next to Lizzie's, Maria was yawning, too. And when Lizzie looked at her friend's worksheet, she saw that Maria was also drawing pictures of Bandit. Maria was better at drawing dogs. Her pictures showed Bandit's whole body. Bandit sitting, Bandit running, Bandit lying on a heart-shaped dog bed. Lizzie smiled at her friend. "Those are really good," she said.

An aide from the office came into their classroom and handed a piece of paper to Mrs. Abeson. Lizzie saw her teacher read it, then thank the aide. Then Mrs. Abeson looked straight at Lizzie.

"Lizzie, Maria, can you come up here for a second?" She waved them up to her desk.

Lizzie looked at Maria. She felt her stomach clench up into a tight knot.

"Your mom called," Mrs. Abeson said to Maria. "She asked me to give you a message from your uncle Teo. It's about Bandit."

CHAPTER TEN

Lizzie grabbed Maria's arm. Maria stared up at Mrs. Abeson, speechless. "What does it say?" Lizzie asked. "What does it say?"

"He's fine," Mrs. Abeson said quickly. She knew all about Bandit, since Lizzie and Maria had shared stories about him many times over the last week. "He made it through the operation just perfectly, and now he's resting comfortably." She checked the note. "It says here that Maria's uncle Teo will be bringing Bandit back home in about four days."

Lizzie leaned into Maria, sighing with relief. "Yes!" Lizzie whispered. "He's okay. He's going to be okay." Maria nodded happily, and they grinned at each other.

"Um, you can let go now," Maria said.

"Oops," said Lizzie. She looked down to see that she was still gripping Maria's arm. "Sorry."

They went back to their seats, but the bell rang before they could finish their worksheets. As they lined up to go out to recess, Lizzie tapped Maria on the shoulder. "There's something I have to tell you," she said. It was time to come clean. Time to tell her friend the truth.

"What?" asked Maria. "Something about Bandit?"

"No, something about me. Something about the dogs I've been walking." They were outside now, over by the swing set. Lizzie sat down on one of the swings, and Maria took the next one over. Lizzie twisted around, spiraling the swing's chains as she tried to figure out how to say what needed to be said.

"You mean, about the dogs you've been walking over on Sunset?" Maria asked.

Lizzie picked up her feet and let her swing spin back around until she felt dizzy. She put her feet down and stared at Maria. "How did you know that?"

Maria shrugged. "I saw you the other day when my dad and I were on our way to the store. You had a big golden retriever with you."

"Atlas," said Lizzie. She swallowed. "Are you mad?" she asked her friend. "I just . . . I wanted to make as much money as I could, to help Bandit."

"And to prove that your business was better than mine," Maria added. But she gave Lizzie a little smile as she pushed off, letting her swing fly. "I *knew* it," she said. "I knew you wouldn't be able to resist making it into a contest."

"I—" Lizzie shut her mouth. "I'm sorry," she said, instead of trying to defend herself. "You were right. And you know what? I have too many dogs to walk. I could really use some help. I could really use *your* help."

The next four days flew by. Walking dogs after school every day was a *lot* more fun when you did it with a friend. Once Lizzie had confessed to Maria, they decided to merge their two businesses into one. They were known as the AAA Dynamic Dog Walkers, and they walked all their clients' dogs together, even Ginger the slowpoke.

Now, on Friday night, Lizzie and Maria sat in Maria's room, waiting for the arrival of Uncle Teo and Bandit.

"When did he say he'd get here?" Lizzie asked for the tenth time, as she jumped up to look out the window.

Maria rolled her eyes. "After dinner. That's all he said."

"We had dinner an hour ago." Lizzie bounced up and down on the bed, knocking over three of Maria's stuffed horses. Maria's room was as full of horse pictures, horse toys, and horse books as Lizzie's room was with dog things.

"Lizzie, calm down." Maria put the horses back in place. "They'll get here when they get here."

Lizzie made a face. "You sound like my mother." Then she jumped up again. This time she was positive she had heard the rumble of a big engine, just outside. "Listen. What's that?" She ran to the window. "It's them. They're here!"

She and Maria flew down the stairs and out the door with Mr. and Mrs. Santiago right behind them, just in time to see Uncle Teo climbing out of the truck's cab, carrying Bandit. The puppy looked tiny in the big man's arms. Uncle Teo smiled at the girls. "Here he is," he said. "Good as new."

Lizzie and Maria crowded around Uncle Teo, cooing over Bandit and reaching out to pet his ears and let him lick their hands. "Is he really okay?" Lizzie asked.

"He really is," said Uncle Teo. "In fact, he's *better* than okay." He smiled down at the puppy in his arms. "This dinky dude is something else."

"What do you mean?" Lizzie asked.

Uncle Teo shook his head, still smiling. "On my way back, I stopped for a bite to eat. Bandit was in the truck—I thought he was asleep on his bed. But when I was paying my bill, I heard barking from outside. I ran out, and there was Bandit, yapping his fluffy head off at a guy who was trying to steal gas out of my truck's tank. Just a few days after heart surgery, and the little guy is scaring off robbers!"

Bandit let out a little yip right then.

I told him a thing or two, didn't I?

Lizzie and Maria laughed. "I'll have to add that to our flyer," Lizzie said. "'Good watchdog.' Maybe now somebody will want to adopt Bandit."

Uncle Teo cleared his throat. "Actually, somebody does." He grinned sheepishly. "Me. I think he'll make a great copilot. It turns out that the fluffball is pretty good company." He squeezed Bandit tighter, and Lizzie saw the palm trees on his arms wave in the breeze.

"Really?" asked Maria. "That's great, Uncle Teo! That means we'll get to see Bandit all the time, whenever you visit."

Lizzie saw the way Uncle Teo was looking at Bandit. It was obvious that the big man had finally fallen under the tiny dog's spell, just like everyone else. And Bandit would have a life of adventure on the road, meeting people all over the country and seeing new places every day. Bandit had found the perfect forever home.

"Now all we have to do is finish making the money to pay the animal hospital for his operation." Lizzie sighed. It was going to take many months of dog-walking to pay that bill.

But Uncle Teo grinned. "I think you might be surprised. Remember Mrs. Kenyon, at Al's Truck Stop? She has been very, very busy raising money from every one of her regular customers. She asked me to bring you both, and Bandit, over to Al's for breakfast tomorrow. She's got a pretty big check waiting for us. I think once we add in what you girls have been earning we'll be just about there."

"Yay!" yelled Lizzie and Maria.

*   *   *

Lizzie rubbed her stomach. Oh, boy! Another breakfast at Al's. "This time I'm going to"—she was about to say "eat all my pancakes," but then she looked over at Maria—"order the short stack," she finished instead, smiling at her friend.

PUPPY TIPS

Taking care of someone else's pet is a big responsibility. If you want to be a dog walker or a pet-sitter, it's important to make sure you understand everything about the animal's personality and special routines.

When I dog-sit my friend's dog Woofy, I have to give him five special pills and two special powders every night with his dinner! When I walk another friend's dog, Sofie, I have to remember that she knows how to squirm out of her collar. And Buddy, a cat I have taken care of, only likes a certain kind of food, served in a certain dish.

Most pets are happiest and safest if you take care of them the same way their owners would.

Dear Reader,

My very first job, when I was about ten years old, was walking the neighbor's dog. Every day after school I would go next door to pick up Sable, a beautiful collie, and walk him around the block. I got paid 50 cents for each walk. Luckily, Sable was very well-behaved and never even pulled on the leash. I'm not sure if I could have managed five dogs at once, the way Lizzie did!

Love from the Puppy Place,
Ellen Miles

P.S. For double the amount of adorable pups, check out THE PUPPY PLACE SPECIAL EDITION: CHEWY AND CHICA!

THE PUPPY PLACE

DON'T MISS THE NEXT PUPPY PLACE ADVENTURE!

Here's a peek at COCOA!

"A puppy?" Charles felt his heart skip a beat. "What about a puppy?"

"I'm trying to figure that out." Dad stopped on the sidewalk, staring at the screen of his phone. "These messages are all jumbled. Meg seems to be trying to tell me that —"

"Dad!" Charles tugged on his father's sleeve.

"Hold on, bucko," Dad said, still toggling away at his phone. "Let me just —"

"But, Dad, look! Isn't that Meg? With that dog?" Charles pointed up the street. A big, strong dog dragged a woman up the street, pulling her like a boat tows a water-skier. Charles noticed the dog's beautiful brown coat and thought that it must be a chocolate Lab, because it looked just like Zeke and Murphy, Harry and Dee's dogs.

"Yeeeooww!" yelled Meg. "Sorry! Sorry!" she said, to the other people on the sidewalk, as she ran along behind the dog, barely missing a lamppost, a mailbox, and a fire hydrant.

Dad had finally let his phone fall to his side, and he stared openmouthed as Meg and the dog charged closer. "I guess that must be the puppy she was writing about," he said.

"Here, pup," said Charles, as the dog approached. He squatted down and held his arms open and the dog barreled into him, knocking him over. Then, as Charles lay laughing on the sidewalk, the dog licked every part of his face: his chin, his mouth, his cheeks, his nose, his closed eyes, his forehead, and even his ears. Charles laughed even harder because it tickled so much. When he opened his eyes, he saw the dog standing over him, grinning a doggy grin and panting happily. Her big thick tail bashed Dad in the knees with every wag.

"This is a *puppy*?" Dad asked Meg, as he bent to pat the dog's head.

Meg laughed. "Well, yes. She's only about a year old. But I have a feeling this dog will be *acting* like a puppy for a long, long time."

"She's beautiful," said Charles. He threw his arms around the dog's strong neck and kissed her silky soft ears. Her glossy coat was the exact color of a Kit Kat, Charles's favorite chocolate bar. But she didn't smell like chocolate. She smelled deliciously of dog. Her yellowish eyes were bright, her ears were alert, and her brown nose twitched and shivered, working overtime to sniff out all the good downtown smells. She had long, gangly legs and huge, chunky paws, and she was at least twice as big as Buddy. "What's her name?" he asked Meg.

"Cocoa," said Meg.

When the dog heard her name, she whirled around and jumped up excitedly onto Meg, making her stagger backward into Dad. "Whoa, there," Dad said as he helped Meg stand upright again. "This dog sure does have a lot of energy."

Charles squatted down on the sidewalk again to try to calm Cocoa down. He gave her nice, long pats the whole length of her body; that usually worked for Buddy when he was overexcited.

"Tell me about it," said Meg, sighing. "That's why we need to find her a home — fast. I already have my hands full with my two dogs. I can't handle this one, too."

"A home?" Dad asked.

Charles felt his heart skip another beat. Maybe Cocoa was going to be their next foster puppy!

"Didn't you get my texts?" Meg said.

"I was just trying to read them, but I couldn't quite —"

Meg waved a hand. "I know. I was kind of in a hurry. Anyway, here's the story. This pup belongs to an older couple, Ernest and Charlotte Thayer, out on Franklin Street?"

"Judge Thayer?" Dad asked.

"That's right, he used to be a judge. He's retired now. He and his wife are both pretty frail, but they still manage to live in their own house and take care of themselves."

Charles wasn't sure what "frail" meant, but he had a feeling it was the opposite of the way Cocoa was.

"And?" Dad asked.

"And a couple of hours ago, the dog came running toward Ernest, banged into him hard, and broke his leg," Meg finished, all in a rush. "I was one of the EMTs on the call, and it was obvious that Charlotte was not going to be able to take care of this puppy on her own. Anyway, Charlotte came with us in the ambulance, so there wasn't going to be anybody at home with the dog, so —"

"So you brought Cocoa along, too?" Dad asked.

Cocoa's head snapped up when she heard her name, but Charles still had his arms around her, so she didn't jump onto Dad. "Good girl, good girl," he whispered into her ear.

Meg nodded. "She rode right up front in the ambulance, with Ted. I couldn't figure out any other way to deal with the problem. And now —"

Dad made a face. "I get it. Now you want us to take this crazy mutt."